Clint Faraday
Book thirty seven
SCREAM MUDDY MURDER

Clint has just arrived in Cusapín. He gets a call from Tonio, in David. There was a scream in the wee hours, about three thirty, from the Muddy River in Pedrigal. A man's body was found on the muddy bank. He had been electrocuted, it seemed.

There? There was no electricity on that side of the river!

Contents

About the author

CD Moulton has traveled extensively over much of the world both in the music business, where he was a rock guitarist, songwriter and arranger and in an import/export business. He has been everything from a bar owner to auto salvage (junkyard) manager, longshoreman to high steel worker, orchid grower to landscaper, tropical fish farmer to commercial fisherman. He started writing books in 1983 and has published more than 350 books as of January 1, 2023. His most popular books to date are about research with orchids, though much of his science fiction and fantasy work has proven popular. He wrote the CD Grimes, PI series, and the Det. Nick Storie series, Clint Faraday series, and many other works.

He now resides in Gualaca, Chiriqui, Panamá, where he writes books, plays music with friends, does research with orchids and medicinal plants. He has lately become involved in fighting for the rights of the indigenous people, who are among his closest friends, and in fighting the extreme corruption in the courts and police in Panamá.

He offers the free e-book, *Fading Paradise*, that explains what he has been through because of the corruption.

CD is the discoverer of the Chadam Protocol for curing cancer.

Facebook page Ambrosia peruviana for cancer.

<u>*An Early Phone Call*</u>

Clint Faraday, retired PI from Florida, declared (to his great pride) Ngobe, put his son down to let him run down toward the clean beach in Cusapín, Comarca Ngobe Bugle, Panamá, just as the dawn was breaking. His beautiful young wife, Tyna, brought him his second cup of coffee. He heard his cellular buzz and sighed. Here for ten lousy hours and they already found him. Tyna called that it was Tonio, whoever that was.

Clint didn't expect that. He took the call.

"Clint? I know you just left here, but we have a sort of odd problem you might find interesting.

"Lilia Suarez called the local station in Pedrigal this morning about three thirty AM. She lives on the Muddy River just above the marina. She'd heard a terrible scream. She wouldn't have been very worried if it had been a woman's scream, but it was a man. It wasn't the kind of thing she could just ignore. It wasn't a regular kind of scream."

"So? Why tell me? What do you mean, it wasn't a regular kind of scream?"

"There's a body. A man's body. It's on the mud bank across the river."

"And?

"He was electrocuted."

"So? He grabbed a wire he thought was a rope or something and it was a hot wire. It was dark."

"The ME says it was a very high amperage shock. It left extensive burns. It was not from some two forty volt line, which there are none of on that side of the river. There's no electricity on that side of the river. Its kilometers of mangrove swamps. It's like he got hit by lightning."

"And he wouldn't have been able to scream if he'd grabbed a hot wire."

"He didn't grab a wire. The point of damage was on the side of his neck."

"Information on the vic?"

"We're not sure, yet. One officer thinks she's seen him around at times. One of the odd job people. Cut grass. Minor repairs, that kind of thing."

"I'll come if you send the chopper. I ain't about to take any long bus ride to David."

"It's on the way. I sent him ten minutes ago. I knew you'd help with this one!

"Thanks, Clint."

Clint rang off and sighed heavily. Tyna, heard the remark about sending the chopper. She said, "Damn it, Clint! We just got here!"

He shook his head. "This is an odd one. You

know how I am. I won't be long, I hope. I'll take clothes for three days."

Nito, his two year old son, ran in with a pan of eggs he gotten from the nests under the porch. Tyna said she thought he had better sense than to run with eggs. He laughed and handed them to her and went to Clint to ask if he was going away again already.

"For a couple of days. You have to take over for me while I'm gone. You're the man of the house when I'm not here."

"Hard job! I have to lay around in the hammock and drink chicha! I can't do the sex parts. She's my mother and I'm not old enough, anyhow."

Clint tousled his hair and hugged him. He tried to picture a two year old in the states saying that. He couldn't.

They played and teased until they heard the chopper coming. He grabbed his bag, kissed his wife and son goodbye and got aboard.

Clint got off the chopper across from the local police station. It took off as he went to the front door, where Tonio was waiting. Tonio said he had to get back to David, that he was called in because of the unusual circumstances here. Raul Amoroso would be officer in charge, but understood they were to give him exceptional privileges.

"Raul? Used to be in Puerto Armuelles? I've worked with him. Good man.

"So?"

"Just what I told you. He was apparently Pedro Pajaros. A sort of general handyman. A few petty theft charges. Nothing serious. Got drunk until he passed out about once a month. A typical street person in the area. No address. Thirty eight. Flako. Bad teeth."

"You just described two hundred people in the area!"

"Exactly. This doesn't make any sense whatever to me."

Capt. Raul Amoroso came out and shook hands. "Emilia Estevez, at the church, said God would strike him dead one day for his blasphemy. Looks like that's our only suspect at the moment."

"Damn! We'll never get a conviction on this one!" Tonio cried, then grinned. "I'll have to get back downtown. It's up to you – thank God!"

They both gave him the finger. Clint and Raul went inside where there was a pot of strong rich coffee. Raul told Clint what they knew, which Tonio had pretty much covered. Clint saw the pictures from many angles. The body was at the morgue. Dr. Garcia was doing a complete.

They walked to across the river from where the body was found.

"Where does the Suarez woman live?" Clint asked.

"Up by the bend there." He pointed toward the marina. "I waited to talk to her for you to arrive. You'd know more what to ask."

"Not much. She heard a scream. I have to know why she thought it wasn't, as Tonio related, 'A regular scream.' It could be important."

Raul nodded. They went to Lilia Suarez's place. She was a middle-aged darker woman, plump, on the edge of being fat, black hair with streaks of gray. She invited them in and showed them the view of the river from her back porch.

"Sra. Suarez, you described the scream as not being a regular scream, and by a man. What did you mean? Did you see or hear a boat at the time or soon after?" Clint asked.

"Call me Lilia. Everyone does.

"The scream was ... I don't know. Could you understand if I said it was pure terror, that it made me get chills and the hair stood up?

"No, other than the fishing boats that ... the tide was going out. No. None. The Indios in their cayucas wouldn't make any noise. They are very quiet while they steal anything they can reach!"

Clint bit his tongue. "I'm Ngobe. Pedro wasn't an Indio and had charges of theft filed against him several times. We Ngobe would never condemn all Latinas because one of them stole something. Any group has thieves!"

Raul was nervous. Lilia didn't seem to notice. "Pedro?"

"Pedro Pajaros, the dead man," Raul replied.

"But ... isn't he that skinny man who cuts grass along here?"

"Yes."

"But ... he was over in that yard by the marina yesterday afternoon. I went for fish from Padi. He was there about six o'clock. Why would he be in the river at night?"

"Yard by the marina?" Clint asked.

"Yes. Where they repair those big boats. They have that big ugly thing for sale. Three years! They should put it in the water. It looks ugly on that rack! In the water it would look like a regular boat!

"Ngobe? You sure don't *look* like any Indio!"

"I have the great honor of being declared Ngobe by the councils on two parts of the comarca."

"Er, I see."

"You didn't see or hear anyone on the river at the time. Just the scream?" Raul asked.

"Yes. Only the scream."

"Well, we thank you for your cooperation. We have to get back to the station. Clint is a famous detective who helps in many very difficult and important cases."

"Somebody killing Pedro Pajaros, a chulo, (bum) is an important case?"

"Any death is important, not only the rich," Clint answered. "Thank you for your help."

"But he was a chulo!"

"He was a person," Clint countered. "He came into the world with nothing and left the world with nothing. That's the truth of any of us, from the richest person on Earth to the most miserable. What we have between birth and death is what's important for one second, then is gone. All we leave is a legacy. Very few leave a legacy worthy of mention ten years later. 'He made a lot of money' isn't one of them."

She looked thoughtful, then grinned. "I think I

respect you quite a lot. I don't like you, but I respect you."

"You liked me until I said I was Indio?"

She looked thoughtful again. "Yes. It was how I was taught. You don't need to say how sad that is. I think I see it – for the first time."

They left.

"Well, I'm proud of you! You could have really gotten off on a tangent there and screwed it up, but you won her respect. I think you actually did get through to her!" Raul said.

"Respect is earned, not given," Clint replied, grinning. "She has to hate herself for respecting an Indio. She'll tell herself I'm not a *real* Indio, so it's alright. Maybe she could've been changed twenty years ago. She can't now.

"I'm interested in that yard by the marina. If he was there as it was getting dark, she had a point. Why would he be on the river at night?"

It was Raul's turn to look thoughtful. "Because he found something at that yard and was taken to the river? There were no boats."

"She didn't actually look. She was scared of what she might see. There were no *power* boats."

"No. There were no boats *using* power. That electricity bit means there was power of some kind!"

"Did anyone else hear the scream?"

"I have two officers going along there, asking."

They went back to the station. Half an hour later the two canvassing officers came in. Only one person might have heard a scream. He couldn't sleep and was watching television. The scream could have been on the TV, he was dozing, but it woke him up. It didn't seem part of the show he was watching.

Clint and Raul went to ask the gringo. He was sleeping and only half-awake when he came to the door.

"Hell! I can never sleep at night and can't stay awake in day. Come on in."

He went in and they went back to the kitchen. There was a porch facing the river and a barge by the shore. Kevin, the man, said he was trying to sell the boat for the person who owned the house. He was a diesel mechanic and had gotten it to working.

"My officer said you may have heard a scream this morning early?" Raul asked.

"Oh, that. Yeah. I'm not sure."

Clint was looking at the spot across the river to the right where the tape was on the mangroves.

"You can see it from here."

Kevin came out. He'd gone to sleep about five and didn't know anything since then until the cops came to ask if he heard a scream. He had no idea a body was found there.

"Try to remember exactly what you heard and if you saw anything or heard anything else," Clint suggested.

Kevin looked thoughtful. "Not really. I was watching a porn movie and was half asleep. I woke up and thought there was a scream, but wasn't sure. I didn't hear anything else."

"No other boats? No voices?"

"I didn't go out. I was in the TV room."

"Did you know if...." Raul started.

"Wait! There was a flash! I thought someone was taking a flash picture on the river. It reflected off the door!"

"A flash?" Raul asked.

"Yeah. Like a flash picture. Real bright for a flash. From back here."

"You're sure it was from back here?" Clint asked. Kevin took them to the TV room. A flash out front wouldn't be reflected where he could see it. The hall led to the kitchen and to the porch.

"It wasn't direct," Clint stated.

Raul went to the kitchen and stood looking around. There was a large silver refrigerator by the hallway entrance in the kitchen.

"There's a direct to the side of that refrigerator with only a little foliage between. A very bright flash would reflect off the fridge down the hall."

Kevin looked and nodded. "What was the flash about?"

"Murder," Clint answered.

"Well, we have a real dilemma in one way," Raul said.

"Which is?"

"No power boat."

"Oh, that. It's easy to figure and tells us where to look."

"You're joking, right?"

"No. What kind of power is being studied for boats that's silent and efficient? What kind would have that kind of amperage on board?"

"An electric boat? It's true they are studying them, but they are too heavy for the batteries to be of more than local use. It would be run on a generator that would make noise, if not much."

"I was a kid when we went to Cypress Gardens, in Florida. We rode in efficient electric glass-bottomed boats. Nineteen sixties."

"So! Where we look is where Pedro was last night! That repair yard!"

"We look anywhere there's an electric boat being designed and built or repaired. The boat may have a generator aboard, but it will still run on batteries at times, so would be silent. Turn off any lights and move unseen on a river at three in the morning.

"I'm looking for the boat to see what else is being researched on it. Nobody would be killed because of just the boat. They've had them for decades."

"An atomic boat would not be so small. They have them, but they must be registered and are much too expensive for anything around here.

"True, such a thing might not be registered.

"Fuel cells? It is possible, but I do not believe they would produce that kind of wattage. This was a lot!"

"You keep up with that kind of thing?"

"I try to not be too far behind in science. Too often it affects my work. Criminals are quick to use new things."

They went to the boat repair yard. No one was around except an old man who was only there to watch the place at night. He slept on the old boat for sale. It was a much better apartment than he could find on what he could make and they paid him two dollars a night for food.

He was bleary-eyed and wobbly.

"Seco or ron for food?" Clint asked.

"Cual quiere."

He hadn't seen or heard anybody around last night. He didn't know if anything was there at six o'clock. He was visiting friends from about two o'clock and didn't pay attention to the rich snobs who came and went. It wasn't his job to pay attention.

When they went down to the hoist Clint said, "He wouldn't hear or see a drummer's parade. The only reason he can keep the job, such as it is, is that he's on the boat. Everything else is too bulky or too heavy to steal."

Raul agreed, "But he has to stay reasonably sober when there's an expensive boat here. Those people learn how to control it. If they don't they sleep on old cardboard boxes behind a bar or something.

"It does tell us no such boat was here."

"No. It tells us no such boat was here after dark last night."

"Clint, the fact he was here doesn't mean what we're looking for was. It was much later when he was over there. You go from here to the marina, then around to where the body was found."

They walked the road to the marina. They went off the road where they could all the way back to the Suarez house. There was nowhere they could see where anyone could get on a boat. There were two teenage boys carrying fish they had caught in the river. They said there were two places where there was a little path through the mangroves. It was hard to get through, but the fish came to the shallow bar. No, it was too shallow for a boat to go in and wasn't in the water at low tide hardly at all.

"There or the marina is what we have. Would they let Pedro hang around the marina?"

"I imagine he cut grass there and around the fence back to the repair yard. Maybe the repair yard, too. He could go on the property if he was sent out to buy supplies or something. He would carry things from the taxis onto the boats, almost always with the boat's owners leading him. They wouldn't allow him aboard if he wasn't doing something for them. Most of those laborers will pick up small items if they're not watched."

"I can picture a scenario where he carried something from a truck or taxi aboard a boat and saw something he wasn't supposed to see."

"It would be noted at night if he went aboard a boat and didn't come back. The gate guard would probably have gone with them, at least to the dock, to be sure he didn't go onto another boat before he left.

Clint looked thoughtful, then nodded. "I'll go back and look at those paths the kids use. He might have been met at one of them when the tide was higher. It was low and going out when he was killed. If it was at the water line at that time it was about an hour and a half to lowest tide, which made dead low tide at about four thirty. The tide was almost back to the body when he was found.

"Right?"

"Dead low tide there was at four forty seven. It's about right."

"Did Pedro use a cayuca?"

"Not that I know of."

Clint said he would check the paths to be sure, then would want to get some information from the marina. He went down the first path. It wasn't easy to navigate, but he could have gotten in carrying something fairly small. The second was a little harder.

He went back to the first and checked the path carefully. There were the footprints of the two boys and the footprints of two larger and heavier people. The boys were both in and out, the others, only one was both ways.

Clint called Raul, who gave him Dr. Garcia's number.

"Were Pedro Pajaros' shoes unmatched?" he asked.

"What do you mean? His shoes?"

"Was one smooth and one a car tread design?"

"Yes. Why?"

"I begin to wonder! That was the one that came back!

"Dr., I thought I'd found the place where ...

something is very odd here!"

"Other than this question?"

Clint laughed. "I'm trying to find where Pedro got on the boat. I found a path he went into, but he came back out. Another person went in and did not come back out."

They talked a little more. Clint thought, then followed the path to the water. There was a mud bar just out from the mangroves. It was almost high tide and the bar was only inches under the water. The old stumps and a few posts were all that let him know the bar was there.

He went back and studied the path. Pedro didn't come all the way. He came to about ten meters from the water, then went back. The other set went all the way to the water.

Clint called Raul and had him bring Plaster of Paris. They took casts of both sets of prints.

"It would appear that was where Pedro saw something," Raul said.

"No. I think he saw something on a boat and followed someone here where he saw what got him killed."

Raul nodded slowly. He sighed. "We have some very sinister plot engaged here. I begin to fear what it might be. Dr. Garcia said the charge that killed Pedro Pajaros was no less than a moderate lightning strike. There was no lightning here last night. Do we have some mad scientist or voodoo priest who can control lightning?"

"I wish I had a clue. At least, a better clue than we have. I want to talk to someone at the marina. I think a friend I helped on a case is there now.

"Raul! I want to talk to the gate guard!"

"Who will have noticed who Pedro was with. I thought of that. Pedro took several things in for several people. There was someone with him all the time, so not much attention was paid to who they were. He believes there were two or possibly three times when he brought the things and was accompanied to the boats by others who have boats here. Most of them knew and used him."

"Shit!"

"Exactly."

They went back toward the marina. Raul got a call and said he had to get to the station. Clint went on. Harry, his friend, was there, They chatted, but Harry had been on Isla de Coiba until yesterday afternoon and didn't know much about what was happening at the marina.

Clint went down to the docks with him to look over the boats. The dockmaster said he didn't monitor the boats after five or before seven, so didn't know if any of them had been out last night.

They looked over the boats there. None of them

had left yesterday. All had been there for at least four days. Most were regulars that came regularly. One was first time. Four were second or third time.

The first-timer was a white forty six foot diesel-powered ClasiCraft. It hadn't been on that river at low tide. Period.

One was a thirty two foot Harborcraft. Probably not, but possible.

One was a thirty six foot Yankee Mariner. Also diesel. Very possible

One was a sleek forty six foot Beachcomber. It would be Clint's first choice. It was quiet and low draft and highly maneuverable.

One was a much older type he couldn't identify. Maybe a homemade. Thirty two foot. Lumpy looking. Maybe the Beachcomber just became second choice!

Those were the ones he would concentrate on. All had outboard auxiliary motors for emergency use. They were expensive four stroke motors that would possibly be quiet enough to not be heard. All had the general accessories. Water tanks were built into most of them, but the homemade had two blue fiberglass two hundred gallon tanks and the Yankee Mariner had one on the cabin roof.

They all needed investigation.

<u>*Shocking!*</u>

Clint went back and suddenly stopped. He still had to find where Pedro got on that boat.

He went back to the second path and along it until one of the muddy spots. There were no footprints in the mud. Nobody had come in there recently.

He walked back toward the Suarez house. There didn't seem to be anywhere.

He had seen something. What was it? It was a bit of a nag. It was while ... at Kevin's place. On the back porch. There was a small malecón that was surrounded by muscle shells. The entire shoreline in back of the place was covered in the shells. He could assume the commercial clam diggers used the place. They dumped the shell around as fill. A boat could come there and return the few hundred meters to where the body was found.

He went to the place. There was a black man standing on the dock who said people came and went there all the time, night and day. Nobody paid them any mind. Yes, Pedro would come there to watch the river and to get a few cents to take the cleaned clams to the distributor.

Pedro had seen something on a boat and had followed someone from it to that path. Something happened on that path. The man met a boat and got aboard. Pedro felt it was not a good idea to be seen there and had gone to the clam dock. The boat had picked him up there.

By arrangement? Because they saw him there?

They had taken him across the river and killed him.

Something was missing. Something very big.

Why did he get on the boat if he'd seen something earlier that scared him off? Would he stay on the dock while the boat came in?

This wasn't coming together at all. Something important had happened between the time Pedro had followed someone into that path and when he got on that boat. Something was out of sequence.

Go over it. Time? Was that it?

Okay. Pedro followed someone into that path and had seen something. He went back out to the road and to the muscle dock. The boat came ... that had to be it. It wouldn't take the boat nearly as long to reach that dock as it would take Pedro.

This fit better. Pedro had gone out to the road and to the dock where the boat was waiting.

The time fit, but he wouldn't go to the boat if he'd seen something that scared him. That meant someone from that boat was already there, waiting. He was forced aboard. He hadn't yelled or anything then, so was probably at gunpoint.

He was now aboard.. They took him across and made him get out. He was killed.

That didn't make any sense, either. Up to the point he was aboard fit very well. Taking him across and making him get out made no sense.

Figure the scream. He had seen something that scared him. He was forced aboard the boat. It moved across the river ... to return to the marina?

Whatever, it was going along close to the far bank when ... an opportunity to jump out. If he could get into those thick mangroves it would be nearly impossible to track and find him.

He was now terrified. He had seen something that meant a real and personal danger.

That possibly meant he hadn't thought he was seen following the person who got on that boat. He had. He went down the road ... Clint called Dr. Garcia.

"How much had Pedro had to drink?"

"Enough to be affected. He drank a lot. You or I would be plastered, but he was probably affected to the point he was feeling no pain or a bit more. Not quite yet to staggering drunk."

"Thanks." So. He was drunk. He probably made some noise or something and they saw him. He was the one who took something to that boat. He was following a person who ... couldn't be seen at the marina?

Whatever, he saw something he was just drunk enough not to notice at the time. He followed the person because he couldn't figure ... that would mean the person was at the marina. It didn't fit again.

Okay. The person was carrying something that could not be seen at the marina is all that fit. He took it onto that boat and suddenly something came together in Pedro's mind. He was scared, so he got out of there. He would be safe so long as they didn't know he had seen. He was going to wherever he was sleeping that night, which meant he passed that spot. Someone was there with a gun. He was forced aboard and they started back toward the marina. They were moving slowly so as not to make any noise. They were close to the far bank because ... the moon was low behind. They were in the shadows of the mangroves very close to that shore. They were distracted for a second. Pedro had jumped overboard and was slogging through the mud toward the mangroves. He was spotted and he ... saw something that terrified him. Probably what they used to kill him. That would mean he saw it on the boat earlier and had an idea what it was or could do. He screamed in that terror and was killed with a bolt of lightning or its equivalent.

That fit. It was probably wrong in detail, but was close in what had happened. It was a matter of finding that boat and what was on it.

Clint went back to the station and told Raul what he thought. Raul agreed it was more than possible. What was seen was probably drugs.

"No. Pedro wouldn't think twice about that. He saw it all the time. It had to have something to do with the way he was killed. That was why the scream. Terror, which means it was something he'd seen demonstrated in some manner. Something ... strange and horrible."

"On the boat. It doesn't make sense. The boat was in the marina at the time. He couldn't have seen something so terrible there. He would have run or reported it or something.

"Your friend, Harry, called. He said to tell you the Anderson boat is leaving this afternoon. They paid for a month and haven't been there nearly that. He thinks you might want to know that."

"The Anderson boat?"

"It is a Yankee Mariner. He said you would know what that means."

"Know anything about the Andersons?"

Raul called the marina and asked for the information. Joseph Anderson was from California. He was forty eight years old and single. He was a structural engineer who worked for NASA until he suddenly quit a year and a couple of months ago, bought the boat, and started traveling around the Pacific along the Americas coast. He was with a man named Carl Gettering, from Germany, about whom nothing was known except he was fifty four and single. He was involved in some kind of advanced laser development and was a photographer.

"If that was done with a laser I could assume a lot and detain him."

"You can hold the boat for something?"

"Hmm. Last port of call, Peru. I think so. I can search the boat for drugs."

"But there won't be drugs on that boat. They shouldn't object."

"And they haven't seen you. I can get a uniform from the storeroom. If you can use some minor disguise we should be able to pull it off. Our only trouble will be that we don't know what we're after."

"If we find something other than drugs, can we use it?"

"Yes. We don't have really stupid restrictions here like in the United States. The warrant will be for all drugs, contraband or weapons. This is definitely a weapon."

"It may not look like a weapon."

"Then it will be a warrant for any *suspected* etc. I can call a damned *screwdriver* a suspected weapon. It is very easily used as one."

"Should do it."

Captain Raul Amorosa and an enforcement officer with the nametag and a bushy mustache, Juan Mendez, both carrying automatic weapons, went along the dock looking for a boat slip number. They came to #23 and Raul called, "Aboard! We will board this boat! Now! All persons aboard will immediately come onto the foredeck for identification! This is the police!"

Two men came to stare at them in confusion. Raul said he was there because the boat had stopped in Peru before coming here. It was a formality, but they were required to search the boat for drugs.

"How very gestapo!" one of the men said. "I am Carl Gettering. This is an outrage! We have no drugs on this craft!"

His Spanish was accented. Clint said, "I agree. The trouble is that the agreement with the gringos says we have to do it. They are interfering here too much."

"Then why do you allow it?" the other said. "I am Joseph Anderson."

"All politics," Raul answered. "We'll try to not

disturb you unnecessarily. The, what they call a 'flag,' is that you have paid for time in a very expensive mooring that you are not going to use."

"I should have thought of that!" Anderson said. "Search away! No drugs have even been on this boat except aspirin and tetracycline!"

"Yes. That and weapons, which you should tell me about if you have any hidden aboard. Most do. It will only mean a fine of twenty five dollars unless they are automatic, which will mean fifty dollars. Other contraband. They expect me to find expensive perfume or that kind of thing to say you have to pay impuestas directly to me of five or ten dollars. I never find that kind of thing even when I find that kind of thing. I think bribery should be prosecuted, not encouraged."

Carl and Joe both laughed. "I don't believe this! I'm dreaming!" Joe cried. "An honest cop – in *Panamá*! Oh, come *on*!"

"It would be funny if it were not so close to the truth. You will find the police on the beat are usually honest, the minor officers sometimes honest, the higher almost never. I become an exception, but I have self-respect, which the ones who are corrupt have no claim to."

"He's also the hardest cop to get around if you've done anything wrong," Clint said. "I don't see anything here on the deck. I'll look inside and on the top."

"The top?" Carl asked nervously.

"An extra large water tank? Drug smuggling? Definitely! It could contain so many things not associated with water in any way."

"Oh. Right. The tank isn't for water. It's a solar collector storage unit."

"A what?" Raul asked.

"It works off the solar panels and stores the charge as electrical capacitance," Joe explained. "It's experimental. Batteries are much too heavy. If we can store the energy in an aluminum capacitor, we save ninety four point four percent in weight over nickel-cadmium."

"I think I read something about that," Clint said. "The trouble was trying to find a way that it didn't discharge totally. It arcs around normal insulation when you try to use it at all."

"Yes. It forms a massive ion flow that we have to learn to control. We can use it when we find that."

"I don't know what that means, but it's okay with me," Raul said. "Juan is always reading that science stuff. It's over my head."

"It's like lightning," Clint said. "It will form an arc to ground if you use any of it. Like that time you were fucking around the TV that never worked right and got a shock when your screwdriver touched a capacitor. That was a little thing. A capacitor smaller than a two centimeter section of a cigarette. The trouble is that the capacitor in the TV discharged all at once. They're mostly used with alternating or periodic current. The minor fluctuations in current in the TV are amplified greatly to produce the sound or movement or whatever.

"Have you considered using the condenser as a base and fluctuating input to take amplification off the output?"

"Yes. It doesn't work because the input would have to be so strong. If it's already that strong, who needs to amplify it any more? We figure we have enough power stored in that capacitor to run the boat for thirty four hours if we can modulate its energy flow. It takes sixty two hours of strong sunlight to charge it that much, but we could use the diesel generator to charge it faster. Electricity is far more efficient than fossil fuels." He seemed to catch himself and said he tended to rant about his favorite project. Raul and Clint went around the boat. There was nothing else to see that was out of the ordinary, but they knew full well that they'd found the murder weapon. It was a matter of being able to prove it. It was also a matter of showing how they did it. It was true there was no way they could show how anyone could direct a lightning bolt. That was certainly what that capacitor would produce!

Clint found a cabinet of tools. There was an electric welder and an acetylene torch. He asked why both?

"Cut with acetylene, weld with electric," Joe answered.

There was what appeared to be a laser projector of some type with a fitting to a cutting torch tip.

"That's a weird one!" Clint said. "What does it do?"

"It can make a very fine smooth cut that wastes nothing and makes a weld easy and smooth," Carl answered. "You focus the laser in the center of the cut and can follow curves and such very quickly. It's much like ... what it accomplishes is adding just enough heat to the acetylene point to allow the laser to make the actual cut, thus it is very thin and smooth."

"Clever!" Clint said. "What'll they think of next?!"

They went back through the salon where a TV set was playing a DVD. It was about lightning. Joe was nervous. Carl said they learned much from the lightning chasers. There was possibly a way to direct an ion flow. That's what happened when they shot the wire into the clouds with a rocket. The lightning followed the wire to ground.

"Of course, what the wire does is form an ion stream around it because of the difference in charge in the wire and the clouds. The wire is disintegrated immediately, in a picosecond, but the ions formed direct the discharge."

"Well, you could use a thin wire to start the discharge ... but it would still discharge at once," Clint said. "You could use it to get rid of trees or whatever that way, but it wouldn't be practical for much else. Maybe smelting platinum or something. It would certainly melt a good-sized lump!

"You couldn't allow air to hit it. Platinum turns black if you get it too hot in air."

They were walking out when a scene came on the TV showing a local house. Raul started to say something, but didn't. They went out. Raul said he would get clearance for them to leave when they wanted within the hour. Joe said he liked the place so much they may stay a few more days. After all! They *had* already paid for it!

When they were away from the dock a bit Raul jumped into the police truck and said for Clint to get in. Fast! He'd seen something!

"What?" Clint asked. "It was while we were leaving? You looked like you wanted to say something."

"That house! Why was it on a DVD of a TV

program from the states?

"For one thing. For the next, that house burned to the ground three days ago. There were two people in it who burned with it. I would say that would be a very good way to hide that they were burned with lightning, wouldn't you?"

Clint nodded. "Maybe that video was on when Pedro delivered something?

"That wouldn't be enough to kill him for when you consider it was just a video of a house that burned down. There's got to be something else on that video. He saw something that connected that video to those people. It was horrible enough that he was terrified enough to jump off the boat and try to get to those mangroves.

"Maybe we can see what else is on it without them knowing. It's a matter of getting on the boat when they're not there. I saw where they have the hidden surveillance cameras and can manage not to be seen on them.

"You have that portable copier for DVDs. I can take it along.

"How do we get them out of the boat for long enough to be sure I can get in, record, and get out?"

"They'll surely get that DVD out of the player by now. I don't think they saw me looking at it. You will need the time to find it."

"That isn't a problem. I notice things."

"Then I'll arrange to let you know when they're not there. They eat at local restaurants every night at seven thirty. I can guarantee no one will see you come and go unless it's another client of the marina."

"An Indio, me, will pass by in a cayuca about that time."

Raul nodded. They went to the station. Raul called a friend to arrange for Clint to have a cayuca handy.

The cayuca came silently alongside the Yankee Mariner and an old Indio slipped silently aboard. Raul had called and said Joe and Carl were with the people from two other boats there at the Mar Caribe, an excellent seafood restaurant near the airport. He would have time. The police officer stationed at the dock entrance would see or hear nothing. The gateman was occupied by a local prostitute who found him *just fascinating*. So strong and so responsible!

The surveillance cameras caught the old Indio by the main port, but he didn't get inside. It was locked.

The lid to the front entrance below was hidden from the camera when the wind blew a piece of palm frond across the lens. The lid was held by an interior lock that was self-locking when it was closed. The thin highly flexible strip Clint slid under the lip quickly released the lock.

He went quickly into the salon and to the rack of DVDs, selected #6-24-pd and slipped it into the battery-operated copier, made a quick copy and replaced the DVD. He checked the TV, which had a copy of the lightning chaser show in the player, but it was the commercial copy.

He didn't stay. He slipped back out, pulled the frond away, then back, then flapped it a few times, then removed it to drop on the lid. He could do that without ever being where the cameras could see him. He went back around and into the cayuca and paddled on up the river.

Back at the (why did I want to say "ranch?") station, he went to the DVD player to slip in the copy he'd made. He and Raul sat back to watch.

It started with a short lecture by Carl about plasma streams. He showed how a stream could be formed inside a tube such as was formed with neon lightbulbs. They would spiral because of the repellant properties of like charges. A maser of certain frequency could be fired down the center and the plasma stream would be concentrated to a very thin straight line. It was interesting and pointed out that the problem outside of a closed vessel was that one had to supply both a positive and negative point that the maser had to be focused very close to.

Next was a short piece about the focusing of electronic beams in a TV. The same problem. You had to have a reception point. You could have many thousands in a small area and could magnetically direct a beam to any of those points.

Next was about capacitance and how to make a capacitor that would contain and store enormous amounts of electrical energy.

There was then a short piece about the nickel-cadmium storage cell that has one serious drawback; it was heavy. Its advantage was that the energy could be "valved" off with resistance and capacity of line so was easily and efficiently usable.

Next was a short TV news feature about a scientist, Dr. Ingrid Gettering, who had been electrocuted under very suspicious circumstances while working with a Dr. Emile Fench and a Dr. Leona D'Angelo. Nothing was known about the incident at that time except that Dr. D'Angelo said Dr. Gettering was working on new types of capacitance directors, which was a science the newswoman knew nothing or less about.

Next was an interview for a small scientific journal with Carl. He claimed that Fench and D'Angelo had stolen Ingrid's invention of a way to valve capacitance and that he believed they had tested the method by killing her with it. There was no other explanation of how she could be electrocuted twenty feet from any electrical line or other source. Fench and D'Angelo had disappeared. He swore to find them and to bring them to justice for his wife's death.

"If he hadn't killed these three here I would not bother to prosecute," Raul said. Clint agreed, but said he wanted to know something about the house fire victim's past. Raul agreed.

Next was the house where the two died. It was easy to identify because of the Chinese Super Mercado a short distance past. It was shown by an approaching camera. A hand knocked on the door, which was unusual here. People called "Buenos!" instead of knocking.

A man answered the door, looked shocked and tried to slam if. The hand pushed the door open and the camera entered to show that the one who answered the door was running down a hallway, apparently calling something. A woman stepped from a side door, looked as shocked, and turned to run. The two ran to the back door, which had a steel barred gate past it that had a built-in lock that the man was trying to fit a key into. He stopped and turned to the camera. The woman was beside him and also turned. You could read her lips. "Please! Please! Oh, please!"

A hand appeared with a five gallon water jug with a strange nozzle on the mouth. There was a pale glow to where the woman had a hand on the man's arm, then bright lightning was flashing and playing on both of them as they gyrated and suddenly dropped, smoldering.

The nozzle was directed at the drapery on the wall, then down the hall and to the bedrooms, where the beds and closets were set afire, then was turned off.

"That jug was sitting under the sink on the boat," Raul said. "I wondered why, seeing as the boat had a water system. I thought maybe mineral water or something.

"I think our victims will be Dr. Fench and Dr. D'Angelo, don't you?"

Clint nodded. "If he'd stopped at that, I'd opt for not solving it. It wasn't Pedro's fault the idiot was playing this when he delivered something to the boat."

"What do you think Carl or Joe was delivering by the river?"

"I don't know except maybe that water jug. If he'd just burned those two and the house he wouldn't want to be seen with it anywhere so he hid it. He saw Pedro noticed the DVD and went after it. There were no gloves on the hands in the picture. He would have his prints identified in a minute. What's inside the jug would tag him.

"You know something else? If he'd strangled Pedro or cut his throat or shot him I wouldn't be adverse to getting minimum. What he did was just plain sadistic. To terrorize him that way isn't excusable.

"He photographed Joe using the thing on Fench and D'Angelo. He watched it, probably over and over. He got a charge out of it. He'll do it more and more if he gets away with this one. I just wonder if Joe is as thrilled."

"I wonder about something else," Raul said.

"What?"

"The hand holding that nozzle was not that of Joseph Anderson's!"

Clint thought. "Too skinny. Too thin. Too dark. It couldn't be Anderson or Gettering."

"It was Gettering taking the pictures. That was his hand on the door and that is very damned professional photography."

"What do we do now?"

"So long as they don't try to go anywhere, let them think they're getting away with it. We still have to be sure that was D'Angelo and Fench."

Clint agreed. Raul went to the computer to ask if his information request was ready. Part of it was. He had it printed out and brought it to spread on the table. Clint looked at the first sheet. "That was D'Angelo."

"But that was *not* Fench!" Raul said, tossing the sheet to Clint. The picture was of a white-haired thin man. The victim at the house was brown-haired and stocky. "In addition, I've seen this one somewhere."

"At the marina?" Clint asked. Raul shook his head. "Not in Pedrigal. In David? I think ... Las Lomas? Between? San Antonio?

"It was San Antonio. Four months or so ago. I was on rotation there because of the Indio thing. He was staying in a house there and came to the meeting where we instructed the people to stay out of the conflict. It was between the Indios and the government. I had the honesty to say that I had my sympathies for the Indios. They had been used and lied to."

"Well, tomorrow morning ... I think I'll go to the Mar Caribe for some seafood now."

Raul nodded and stood. It was across the street from Pedrigal. He would drive Clint to close and Clint could walk over.

At the restaurant Clint saw the party from the marina. The white-haired man was with them. He seemed to be dominating the conversation.

Clint took a table around the partition where he could hear them, but they couldn't see him. He listened to the man telling about his experiences as a college professor in Germany. He had a strong accent and was speaking English.

After a delicious meal and three-quarters of an hour Clint left, thinking Dr. Fench was a boring lecturer with an overblown opinion of himself. Twice he had started to say something about an invention he was going to have patented and Gettering changed the subject.

Maybe Clint had the basics figured, but there were a few details he had missed by a hundred eighty degrees.

Clint had another problem with this stupid mess now. What was Fench doing here, apparently working with Gettering and possibly...? No. That DVD was there. Working with Gettering and Anderson? Who was the man who was killed in that house?

Clint wanted to finish this one today. He was missing his wife and son. He was *not* going to spend so much time away from them anymore.

He went to the police station at dawn. Raul was there and they went to breakfast at the twenty four hour restaurant, then back to the station. He had checked on the victims and found that Leona D'Angelo was in Panamá as Mrs. Robert Evans, originally of Hamburg, Germany, married to Evans in Florida ten months ago.

Robert Evans was checked out and found to be Robert Evans from Indian Rocks, Florida. He went to university in Germany and worked for Fench D'Angelo Laboratories in Hamburg for eight years before returning to Florida after an incident at the laboratories. D'Angelo went with him. He couldn't find much about Fench since he left Germany for England at about the same time.

"This might mean something," Clint suggested, reading the information sheet on the computer screen. "Gettering hampered the investigation of his wife's death. He had filed for divorce more than a month before and they were not living together, which made suspicions find some new directions and muddied the investigation to a point nothing could be proven against anyone.

"I'm beginning to think we were right about Pedro's death and what happened, but not about much else."

"I don't understand D'Angelo's murder now," Raul complained. "The reaction when that door opened was far too shocked to ... he worked at the laboratory. Gettering, him, did not. Gettering was supposed to be looking for her and Fench, Fench shows up with him here, but then she and Evans get killed. Talk about muddy! Was it Evans and D'Angelo who killed Ingrid, not Fench and D'Angelo? Did Gettering find Fench and get convinced he didn't do it?"

"I think Gettering and Fench killed her and D'Angelo and Evans could prove it somehow," Clint said. "It would fit, but how did Anderson get involved?"

"Well, if it's that, Anderson's an engineer and Fench wants a patent on an invention. It will be an invention of Ingrid Gettering."

"And Evans and D'Angelo could screw it up to where they could never get a clear patent. The laboratory was Fench and D'Angelo! The patent for an invention of a deceased employee who developed it while working for that company goes to the company!

"Raul, my friend, this is one greedy bunch of sadistic monsters if there ever was one.

"I think Ingrid was going to divorce Gettering and take her patent with her. The only way they could get that patent ... they didn't know how to make it! They could have filed for the patent as soon as she died, but they didn't know the one important part that would make it work. That nozzle. It was Anderson's engineering that made Gettering and Fench ideas work. That's how he got into it at all. I don't know if it was luck or by plan that he was another greedy sadist, but that bunch fit too well for coincidence.

"We have to have that nozzle and the jug now. We can tag all of them."

"We can get to the boat before they can get rid of anything. There are people watching from all angles."

"I thought to photograph everything in that boat most diligently. I went there while you were in the restaurant with them and entered as a police officer with a warrant. They will see that I did that with their spy cameras I suppose, unless they were attached to the computer there that had an accident. There was no recorder on it except the hard drive, which was erased when a cold half-cup of coffee sitting on the small shelf above was knocked off directly onto the power supply. Bummer! They will have to have the whole thing replaced! Perhaps we can recommend Kelvin?"

Clint laughed drily. "That should light a fire or two!"

There was a sudden fire alarm at the marina. They heard the siren and raced over. It seemed the Yankee Mariner was burning. Anderson was running around screaming about his records. Gettering was screaming about his research. Clint noted how it seemed a bit rehearsed.

"It would seem as though the evidence is going up in smoke," Raul said. "A pity. It was a fine craft. Shall we hear the story?"

They went to Gettering, who was yelling about saving the tank on top. That was a standard type of capacitor, if a very large one, and wouldn't be anything critical. The jug and nozzle were the critical parts. They knew how to make them now, so little would be lost. He wasn't yelling about any of that. Anderson was yelling about saving the computer. It had all his research on it. He would know it was erased. That was what the fire was all about. They knew someone had been there.

"A pity. Well, you can always build another one," Raul said. "That was a fine boat. It's a pity to lose such a craft, but I imagine the insurance will get you another."

"The insurance can't replace the research!" he screeched – a little too high and a little too loud. "I have ten years of work in that computer!"

"You didn't make backups?" Clint asked.

"Of course I did! They're in the bunkroom!

"My dear god! Stop it before it reaches the bunkroom!"

Anderson ran over to screech, "Ten years! We spent ten years on that and it's gone!"

"Ten years, My-my!" Raul said. "You haven't known each other but three or four."

"Er, you see, that is, we were doing individual research in different areas that came together with this," Gettering said, seemed to realize he was suddenly not screeching, and ran off yelling about a file cabinet that was fireproof.

"I guess your collection of DVDs will have melted, by now," Clint said. "Pity. I suppose some of them will be irreplaceable. The ones of your personal projects."

Anderson hid a flicker of a smirk. Clint had

phenomenal side peripheral vision and caught it while he seemed to be looking at Gettering.

Raul's radio announced a call for him. He answered and the voice said that Blanco was loading luggage into his car. He said to detain the subject. Clint could figure what that meant and said, "What was that?"

"Dr. Fench suddenly seems to be planning a trip. Without informing anyone. How thoughtless of him!"

Anderson walked away looking confused and scared. Clint grinned.

"They think we know something, but they also think we can't prove it," Raul said. "They'll try to bluff it out I suppose. That told them they aren't going anywhere."

"It'll be interesting to see if they try."

They stood around looking amused awhile. The fire was stopped, but everything inside was a mess. As soon as it was cooled down enough they went aboard. Raul went to the kitchen sink and said it was very strange! A big coil of aluminum foil and dielectric stripping with melted plastic under the sink. He took pictures of everything. He checked the tool cabinet and called, "Clint! Over here!"

Clint went over as Gettering appeared, coming into the salon. Raul saw him and noted that Clint knew he was there. "It seems they forgot to open the cabinet door. It's made of steel. Very little was damaged greatly in here. That odd laser affair is here. We can take it to the station. I see the acetylene and oxygen cylinders didn't get hot enough to explode. Probably the pressure was low enough to begin with that it didn't reach critical.

"That's odd."

"What?"

"There's no oxygen input into the nozzle. It must be difficult to maintain a fine point to focus the heat for the laser to work.

"What is this? It's not a laser! It's got a coil that seems very ... it's a maser!

"Oh! Dr. Gettering! Would you care to explain how a maser can cut a fine point with unoxidized acetylene forming a focused heat source?"

Kettering turned and stamped out. Clint charged ahead and looked up at the tank on the roof. It wasn't damaged. It was fiberglass. Not much heat had gotten to it. The steel roof protected it from direct flames reaching it. Gettering was doing something at an electric panel.

"The tank!" Clint yelled. "Water on the tank! Fast!"

A fireman with a hose looking for spot fires looked at him like he was crazy.

"Water on the tank! Now!" Clint yelled as Raul

came up and yelled, "That is an order!"

The man turned the hose on the tank. "Top!" Clint yelled just as Gettering got the panel open and threw a breaker. There was a lot of flashing and all of them were knocked off their feet. The man with the hose was wearing a rubber suit, which saved his life. An arc followed the water to the hose and he was knocked unconscious.

Raul was the first to regain his feet. He jumped onto the dock and grabbed the automatic rifle from the police guard there and pointed it at Gettering. Gettering was just managing to get to his feet.

"I won't shoot to kill you. I'll just shoot you in places that will make you beg me to kill you!"

Gettering froze and slowly put his hands up. Raul tossed the police officer his handcuffs and told him to handcuff the prisoner to the metal steps to the flying bridge while they finished their initial investigation.

They didn't find much more. It seemed as though Anderson had disappeared. The guard said he'd gone to the marina offices. There were a lot of people around because of the fire. He had apparently left in a taxi when they started leaving.

"He won't go far. We can take Dr. Gettering to the station for a little intimate chat session," Raul suggested. "I think he won't enjoy it, but that is one of life's little annoyances."

They went to the station where Gettering was yelling that he wanted an attorney present! He demanded to speak with the German embassy! He was being framed! His civil rights were being trampled on! There would be an international incident! Police brutality!

The officer, Lt.Amos Lagos, said in excellent English, to shut up, that he sounded like one of those cheap TV movies. Lagos went out front to file his report.

"I demand to know the charges you brought me here on! This is outrageous!" he yelled.

"Arson. Would you care for coffee?" Raul said calmly.

"Er? Uh? Arson?" he stammered.

"The fire was set in three places. You and Dr. Anderson were the only two aboard. It doesn't take a genius," Raul replied. "Coffee?"

Gettering looked confused and nodded. "Black and strong.

"Arson? That's all?"

"All?" Clint asked. "We don't need more. We can hold you in a cell on that for as long as the investigation takes. If that investigation leads to other charges they can be added."

"You can prove there was arson?" he asked. "I'm just curious. I know I can be held."

"There was a smell of diesel fuel in the salon. The investigator was already there. They have a machine that will identify it in ten seconds. There was no reason for it to be there. It was at all three ignition points, which is another thing. One, maybe you get away with it. Two, not likely. Three? You're gone."

"You trashed the computer?"

"I accidentally knocked the coffee off the shelf. Sorry, but those things happen."

"I see. The drug search thing means you were there with a legal warrant. You didn't take anything. We can't claim it wasn't included on the warrant's wording."

"I took hundreds of pictures. This is not the United States. Anything I find can be used here."

"It isn't about a boat burning. It's about Pedro Pajaros," Clint said.

"That was unfortunate. It was an accident. He fell overboard and grabbed a line to climb back. It was a lead from the tank. I wanted to call the police and report it, but Dr. Anderson said it would compromise our research. The tank was part of it."

"He grabbed a high amperage bare electrical cable with the side of his neck? Really?" Raul asked innocently. Gettering clammed.

"Well, you'll have some explaining to do about

Dr. Fench. You make serious charges that he killed your estranged wife, then show up here and run around to fancy restaurants and so forth with him," Clint said. "Evans and D'Angelo are here and end up dying in a house that burned down because of arson of the type you've demonstrated as an MO that ... no, that wasn't nearly the same. This one was diesel fuel. That one was electrical. Very different, but electrical is your field."

"Er, electrical? Uh! Evans and D'Angelo? Who are they ... okay. I knew them in Germany. I didn't know they were here until I read about the fire."

"Dr. Fench was here. He was the other one in the laboratory when Mrs. Gettering died. Perhaps he is able to use the electrical thing?" Raul asked.

"Yes! That must be it! Fench killed them!"

"Why?" Clint asked.

"My wife! Fench *did* kill her! They knew it! He convinced me they killed her. He said he was afraid of them and ran because they would kill him as well because he could show they killed Ingrid!"

"This is downright surreal!" Clint snarled. "Pick up Anderson and Fench and we can have a little chat with all of them. Maybe one of them can come up with a story. This one isn't cutting it."

"I think that is in order here," Raul replied.

"Everything you say makes sense if you don't hear everything else you say. Now you are left totally without reason for firing your boat."

Gettering looked shocked again. "Uh! Well, you see, Dr. Anderson was doing that when I got up. He said it was to protect the research. I went along."

"Anderson was going to fire the boat while you were asleep on it, but you woke up and helped him?" Clint asked.

"You were all yelling about the fire losing all of your research," Raul pointed out.

"We knew the research was gone. The computer was fried. We can build the collector from what we know. Nothing is really lost. That was to hide that we fired the boat."

"But leaves you without *reason* to fire the boat. Everything you say negates everything else you say. I'd think you would have the intelligence to make up a story before you do something stupid that will result in your needing that story," Raul said.

This time he stayed clammed.

"So. We will bring your confederates here to each accuse the others," Raul said. He went to the radio and said to find Anderson and bring Fench in for questioning.

Fench would be brought in. They would have to

find Anderson. It shouldn't be too hard. There weren't many gringos in Pedrigal. None who looked like Anderson.

Clint spent an hour talking with Tyna and Nito on the cell phone. He and Raul went to lunch and made a loose semi-plan about interrogating their bunch. Raul wanted to show they had the DVD and face them with it. Clint said they would miss too much. They would try to find more. If it didn't work they would bring out the DVD.

Fench was brought in and had his ID checked, then was passed to the interrogation room where Clint and Raul were sitting, drinking coffee. He was nervous and indignant, demanding to know what was going on.

"Have some coffee, Dr. Fench," Raul said. "We have a few questions. You have a good idea what it's about or you wouldn't have been attempting your hasty exit."

He sat and waited. Clint poured him a cup of the coffee and sat back. They let the silence grow for about two minutes, then Clint said, "It seems strange to us that you are here, Anderson and Gettering are here, Evans and D'Angelo are here. Evans and D'Angelo supposedly die in a fire, but their bodies show signs of having died by high amperage electrical shock. Ingrid Gettering died of high amperage electrical shock. Pedro Pajaros died by high amperage electrical shock. Gettering tried to kill several people fighting the fire he set on that boat with high amperage electrical shock. Gettering had made very public statements that you killed his estranged wife, yet he is going to restaurants with you, great pals. Your field is electrical shock, in a manner of speaking.

"Make fifty or sixty questions out of that and try to answer a couple."

"I don't have to answer any questions about anything."

"True," Raul said. "Of course, you have to realize that this is Panamá. You are guilty until proven innocent. You don't answer the questions at your own peril. You can't prove innocence by remaining silent and waiting for us to prove guilt here.

"You are guilty. All we're trying to find is of exactly which parts. To not give that information means you are guilty of all of it.

"We have some evidence that very clearly fixes blame of certain things directly upon you."

"I met with Carl when he first came here and proved to him that I wasn't involved in his wife's death, that it was Leona. We resolved that. The only other times I was involved with any of them at all was social meetings with Joe and Carl.

"Carl called and told me the boat was fired. He didn't know what was going on. I was going to a place to be away from personal danger, if there is any, until this blows over."

"Murder doesn't blow over," Clint said. "Carl Gettering told us he changed his mind about your involvement in his estranged wife's death, that he now believed you were involved."

"So now you're coming after me for something that happened around the world from here?"

"No. Evans, D'Angelo and Pajaros happened here," Raul pointed out. "My personal feeling is that Gettering was the main person involved in his estranged wife's death."

He was silent for a minute. "So. I wondered why you kept stressing that they were estranged at the time of her death. I imagine it is more than possible he was involved. He was very intent upon getting her invention."

"Which you have and have used," Raul said.

"Which I understand they have. Whether or not it has been used is in question here. Not for the purpose we strove toward."

"No. The basic purpose is, as usual, money," Clint stated positively. "You're one greedy bunch."

"That is undoubtably true of all the others. My

interest is in the scientific applications. I have no need of money."

"You want power. Directly," Raul said.

"I suppose I do. Not that I would use the power. I just want to have it."

"I can understand why Ingrid, Leona and Robert were killed, if I don't agree. Pedro Pajaros, I can't understand," Raul said. "He was a local drunk."

"He was nothing. As you say, a common drunk." Fench waved a hand in dismissal.

"I'll be damned! It wasn't Gettering, it was *you*!" Clint exclaimed. "You are one slimy rotten piece of runny shit! You're a pervert of a type I've only seen in TV movies!"

"What do you mean?!" Raul cried. "It was him? What was him?"

"It was him Pedro followed down that path to the river. He was carrying the jug and nozzle. He got on the boat. He knew he was being followed. He knew Pedro wouldn't be suspicious to any great degree when he met him at the clam dock.

"What did you do? Offer him some rum?"

"As you say, he was a drunk."

"So. You got him aboard and showed him a DVD. You were over on the other shore. He saw you carrying the jug and nozzle in that DVD and he saw what you did with it. The DVD was in the player when we went aboard the next morning because you had shown it to him to make him panic and jump off the boat into that mud, which was very good for conductance. You used the thing on him as an experiment or just because you're a true B-movie monster!

"Raul, you took pictures all over that boat! Did you get the engine room?"

"Yes. I've downloaded them. They're in the computer."

They left Fench sitting there with a guard at the door who had orders to shoot him if he even looked like he would move.

They went through the pictures. The fire hadn't reached the engine room. That was why Gettering was trying to throw that switch to the tank. It would probably arc through the device connected to the transmission of the boat. It seemed to be an electric motor with a strange bottle attached to the input lead.

"That was their electric drive motor. It's why Anderson knew exactly how long the tank would run the boat. I don't see how it would work.

"We don't need that now. All we need to know and be able to prove is that it's there. They do have an important invention that would have made them all millionaires. They're all so greedy they wouldn't settle for part of it.

"Let's go back in there. I personally want to use

his own invention on him.

"You do realize that his little lightning machine isn't part of the original invention? He made that deliberately for one purpose and one purpose alone. The Evans and Pedro was what it was for."

Raul sighed very deeply. "No matter. Anderson and Gettering were accomplices. Gettering was there for that video and both of them were there for Pedro."

"I'd like to use the thing on all of them! Maybe a lower amperage that would make it take awhile to burn them!"

Raul shuddered. "Watching that video was like watching those old horror movies where the mad scientist watched people's skin melt from high radiation and such. He can do that or ... I don't think he feels anything at all. To him, it's an interesting experiment he's watching.

"Clint, I'm not equipped to deal with this thing, emotionally. I will feel my skin crawling when we go back in there!

"You told me your friend had made something that would do these kinds of things. It's one thing to talk about it. It's entirely another to see it!"

"No. Dave's invention will shoot down a plane or put a hole through an armor sheet. It isn't something from a horror movie. It's just sort of a gun that will hole anything from a distance. He doesn't have to be where he sees the results, though a hole in a sheet of armor plate could never be called a perverted horror. It amounts to a special gun there's no defense for.

"We have to get Anderson and Gettering here. We're going to show them ... Gettering will have a video of Pedro's death somewhere. He took those pictures of the Evans. He's just as bad as Fench. Anderson watched those things. He didn't react much. He's another pea in that pod.

"Raul, there's no death sentence here. I'd like to see them strapped into an electric chair. It would be a sort of poetic justice."

Clint looked thoughtful. He said he was going to the hotel. Call him when they had Anderson. He wanted to talk to Gettering for a minute first.

He talked to Gettering and told him what they had and that there was no way they would get away with anything. He was guilty until proven innocent and that video was all they needed to destroy any least tiny chance they had. He could depend on spending the rest of his worthless life in solitary confinement.

He did make a video of Pedro's electrocution. He was emotionless about it. It was on the boat and didn't survive the fire. It was still in the videocam. One fire was started in that cabinet because of the film and plastic that would burn fast and hot. It happened about like Clint thought. He was aware they were all insane, but the world was insane.

Clint had wanted to use enough psychology on him that he would induce Fench to use the device on all of them somehow, but it wouldn't work. The device was on the boat. He did want to know how it worked.

Anderson was brought in while he was talking to Gettering. He asked that he be allowed to talk to him for a few minutes.

He asked how the device worked.

"There is a heavy insulated line. It has to be a distance from the capacitor to avoid cross-arcing. We use a fast-pulse motor. There is a spinning resistor block in a cylinder. It has a conductor through it. We can time the spin for, in the case of the boat, eighty revolutions per second. There is a limited discharge each time the conductor passes the input point. It automatically limits the amount of energy flow.

"The problem has always been the arcing of such vast power. The distance and the degree of insulation in the resistor controls it very nicely. We have moved from Peru to here and have used the boat several times to make short tours. We have never used the diesel."

"I meant Fend's little personal execution device

used on Pedro and the Evans."

"Oh, that. It was a difficult kind of engineering. I had to find a way to direct a precise ion stream. It wasn't very difficult after I found the principle.

"You see, the problem was being able to direct the stream to a specific small point. We found a way to focus to a point the size of a dime. Less."

"That's what I mean."

"The piece your policeman friend saw was a maser is that, in a way. It works more like a laser in that it can keep a very fine line of ions ... well, it is very finely powdered iron. Dust.

"The acetylene tank contains the powder under pressure of more than thirty six hundred pounds per square inch. Nitrogen. There is a trigger device. You pull the trigger, it releases the iron dust through the cutting head, which has an extended perfectly straight fine tube leading to it from the acetylene line. At thirty six hundred pounds it delivers the iron powder at a source firing point in an expansion rate from one quarter of a millimeter to one millimeter at thirty meters distance in two thousandths of a second. The trigger contact for the capacitor is timed for that two thousandths of a second. The energy flow is along that ion stream. Very effective and very accurate!"

"I'll say that for it," Clint agreed drily. "I can

suppose there's a use or two for such a thing other than as a weapon."

"None that I know of."

Gods that I don't believe in, but that's one disgusting cold, twisted, sick motherfucker! Clint thought as he left the room.

Clint got off the chopper and told Estefan, the pilot, he could stay there at the house for the night. It was too dark to try to fly back to David. He answered that he could fly at night very well. They had enough light at the chopper field.

Clint went toward the house and was almost bowled over when Nito charged to jump on him and hug him. He held his son and found himself crying. He hoped Nito would never be exposed to anything one tenth as sick and horrifying as what he'd seen in the past three days – that seemed like three centuries.

The reaction hit him solidly for the first time. He clung to Nito and to Tyna, who came to him then, as sobs shook him. They both seemed to understand, though he didn't.

After a few minutes they went on to the house. Tyna said he was never to tell them or anyone what had happened. It was past and gone. They had him back where he belonged, only a little worse for wear.

He went into a strange kind of fog for the night and most of the next day. His subconscious mind took the time to sort things out. He came to terms with it.

Basilio came at dusk to sit with them on the porch to chat. He started to ask Clint about his trip to David. Tyna shook her head slightly so he asked if much had changed there since the few days before when they came back from Tula.

They chatted for awhile until it was dark, then Basilio went home and Tyna, Nito and Clint went to bed.

Tyna was right. It was past and gone. He was Ngobe and able to know that life spent was life spent and could not be gotten back. The past is inalterable.

He remembered the expression Dave had used. "You can't unring a bell." How very true!

The Indio philosophy was that. You had to let such things go. Make them something that you had seen in a movie. You learned what the movie was trying to teach you and filed it away to never bring forth again unless there was a reason.

He turned to hold to Tyna. Nito, his other reason for living, said, "Time for that sex stuff. I'll go to bed!" and laughingly went to his room. Tyna asked, "Is it over now?"

"It'll never be over, but I think I'm past it. I can put it in its place in my mind. I can't say I'll put it in a dark corner because it *is* that dark corner, but

I won't dwell on it. They were the aberration and there's no chance of it happening again. Like Brother Dave said, 'You might do something similar, but you can't do that.' Somebody in the audience yelled, 'Do what again?' He said, 'That.' Something like that. Maybe he said ... what difference does it make?"

He held Tyna, who teased at his chest. He responded. It was a wonderful night after he returned to being Clint Faraday, Ngobe Indio and damned proud of it!

It was three days later when he got a call from Raul. All of them were convicted and sentenced to the maximum.

"And Clint, a thing you started. Gettering and Fench are being transported to Germany to face charges proven here concerning Ingrid Gettering. It will be to Germany to pay for the rest of their disgusting lives!"

Some things work out.

C. D. Moulton's works are available on most major outlets as printed or e-books. CD writes the CD Grimes, PI, mysteries, the Det. Lt. Nick Storie mysteries, the Clint Faraday mysteries, the Flight of the Maita science fiction series, books on orchid culture and many others of many types. Mystery, adventure, intrigue, science fiction, humor, fantasy, paranormal, mild erotica, and factual.